The Zebediah Stowaway

Written by John Parsons

Illustrated by Richard Hoit

Contents

For learning solutions, visit **cengage.com.au**

Meet the Characters

Jeremiah

A boy who finds he has a conscience.

Abby

A girl who often gets the others out of trouble.

Nathan

A boy who loves plans involving escapes and catfish.

Suzette

A girl who sees the best in people.

Mother Hildegard

A nun at the orphanage.

Father Cicatrice

Inspector-General of Irregularities.

Dear Reader

Life at the orphanage becomes very strange for Jeremiah, Abby, Nathan and Suzette when someone gets suspended – and it isn't one of them! But things get even more peculiar when a fugitive stowaway joins them aboard the Zebediah. Things they thought they'd never see start to happen all over the place!

John Parsons
Author

The Orphanage

1. Mother Hildegard's office
2. The nuns' dormitory
3. The underground cellars
4. The orphanage wall
5. The secret tunnel
6. The grassy ditch

1 Suspended!

I knew something was up the moment a line of sombre nuns threaded their way into the classroom, eyes downcast, looking for all the world like a disgruntled black and white caterpillar shuffling towards an unappetising cabbage leaf.

Mother Hildegard, who'd entertained herself for the last ten minutes by furiously colouring in my essay with large red crosses, looked up.

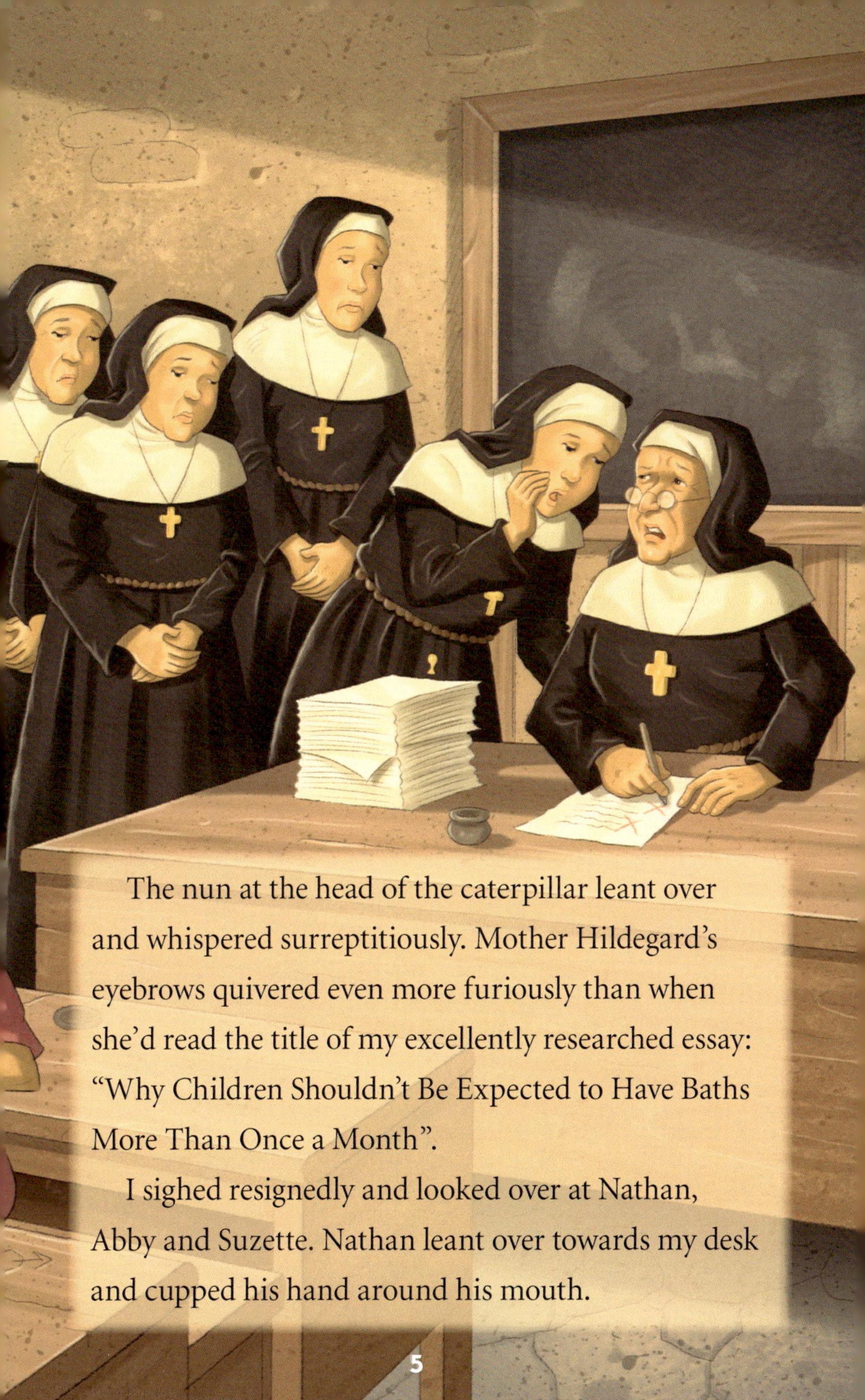

The nun at the head of the caterpillar leant over and whispered surreptitiously. Mother Hildegard's eyebrows quivered even more furiously than when she'd read the title of my excellently researched essay: "Why Children Shouldn't Be Expected to Have Baths More Than Once a Month".

I sighed resignedly and looked over at Nathan, Abby and Suzette. Nathan leant over towards my desk and cupped his hand around his mouth.

"What have you been caught doing this time, Jeremiah?" he whispered.

With nuns, it always pays to be one step ahead, so I immediately started racking my brain. What heinous misdemeanour had I committed in the last three days and, more importantly, what was my plausible excuse going to be? Unusually, my conscience was relatively clear. If you didn't count sneaking up to the nuns' dormitory and swapping glasses of false teeth around, which I'd managed to accomplish last Tuesday night, I was about as innocent as a runaway orphan could ever be. And, let's face it, everyone agreed that watching twenty nuns trying to chew lumpy porridge with oversized, undersized and crooked false teeth on Wednesday morning had certainly been worth it.

"What are you grinning at, Master Jeremiah?" thundered Mother Hildegard. "Didn't you hear me?"

She was standing framed in the classroom doorway, ready to join the tail of the rapidly disappearing caterpillar of nuns.

"Twelve!" I said, using my standard answer to questions posed when I hadn't been listening. It worked

for all kinds of things: how many months were in a year, how many things were in a dozen or how many times I'd been told to do something that I still hadn't done.

"Class is dismissed," hissed Abby from behind me.

"I'm sorry, Mother Hildegaard," I said. "I was thinking about my magnificent essay. Twelve. A perfectly acceptable number of baths to have a year."

Snorting, Mother Hildegard joined the winding caterpillar of nuns disappearing out into the corridor.

I looked at Nathan, Abby and Suzette in bewilderment. What was going on? Not only had class been dismissed, but the unthinkable had happened. I'd actually managed to use the "twelve" answer without having to duck a piece of Mother Hildegard's well-aimed chalk!

Within an hour, the day grew stranger. An assembly was called. Assemblies were never good news, usually being called to announce orphanage rules about wearing socks of the same colour, or earwax and fingernail inspections. Nathan, Abby, Suzette and I took our usual places at the back of the assembly, and I stared glumly at my feet, waiting for the unpleasant news.

The hall fell silent as the nuns entered in single file.

"Who's that?" whispered Suzette. To my surprise, Mother Hildegard was nowhere to be seen. Instead, a stern-looking priest led the solemn procession to the front of the hall, where he turned to speak.

"My name is Father Volto Cicatrice," he boomed theatrically, staring ominously at the assembly. "Father Volto Cicatrice, Inspector-General of Irregularities at Orphanages. Unfortunately, I must inform you that some grave irregularities have been discovered at this orphanage. Grave, indeed!"

The nuns who stood like a zipper to one side of Father Cicatrice clucked mournfully. I stared at Nathan.

"Finally!" I said. "They're going to stop forcing us to eat vegetables, do schoolwork and take more than twelve baths a year!"

"I somehow doubt that," said Nathan, shaking his head. "He's only a father, and I reckon you'd need to be at least a bishop to stop those things."

"SILENCE!" bellowed Father Cicatrice, pointing a crooked finger in our direction. He fixed us with an angry glare, then returned to his speech.

"It has come to my attention that a considerable number of valuables have gone missing from this orphanage," he rumbled. "Until I discover who is responsible, Mother Hildegard has been suspended! She is being accommodated somewhere secure until my inspections are completed."

There was an audible gasp from the assembled children.

"From this moment," continued Father Cicatrice, "I am in charge!"

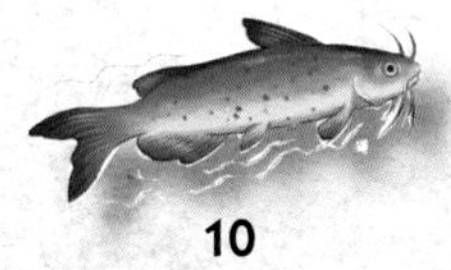

2 A Terrible Dilemma

"I don't believe it!" said Suzette. "It's inconceivable that Mother Hildegard could be under suspicion of stealing valuables."

Two days had passed since the extraordinary assembly, and during that time, Mother Hildegard had indeed vanished.

"She confiscated my slingshot last week," I pointed out. "That was extremely valuable."

Suzette, who was always able to see the best in people, even well-armed nuns, shook her head.

"I don't believe it," she repeated emphatically. "Mother Hildegard may be stern, she may have lots of rules, but she would never contemplate anything dishonest."

"Suzette's right," nodded Abby. "Every time we've escaped from the orphanage and ended up in trouble, she's been there to help us out. I'm certain she's innocent."

Personally, while she still had my slingshot, I wouldn't go that far – but I had to agree it seemed unlikely Mother Hildegard was guilty of any allegations of thievery and misconduct.

"Well, if valuables are missing from the orphanage, someone's a thief," said Nathan. "I wonder who?"

"If we want to clear Mother Hildegard's reputation, we'll have to find out," said Suzette. "But Father Cicatrice seems convinced she's guilty. Where can we go for help?"

I thought for a moment, struggling with a terrible dilemma. On one hand, I could have a blissful life free from Mother Hildegard's quivering eyebrow and well-aimed pieces of chalk. On the other, I could do the right thing.

I'd clearly been around Mother Hildegard far too long, because evidently she'd succeeded in actually giving me a conscience.

"I know what we'll do," I said. "And I know where we'll go." I winked at Nathan, Abby and Suzette, and began to explain my plan. Thankfully, it involved quite a lot of rule-breaking, and Mother Hildegard

probably wouldn't approve, so my recently discovered conscience hadn't entirely taken over.

The good thing about reading and writing lessons was that if you handed in enough cheeky answers, you inevitably ended up with a punishment involving chores no one else wanted in places no one else wanted to go. The next day, when we were supposed to be studying collective nouns for groups of things, I seized my opportunity.

While everyone else wrote down collective nouns like a parliament of owls, a clowder of cats and a skulk of foxes, I constructed my own particularly descriptive and quite original nouns.

A disapproval of nuns. A queasiness of vegetables. A nincompoopery of Inspectors-General.

After reading my list aloud to the class, I found myself that evening with a bucket and mop, staring at the stony floors of the dark, gloomy cellars beneath the orphanage.

A row of wooden doors stretched into the darkness. Old furniture, boxes of junk and dusty books were usually stored behind these doors – but, tonight, I had a suspicion I'd find something else secured down here.

In another part of the orphanage, Nathan, Abby and Suzette were getting ready for our escape. I had to be quick, or we'd find ourselves locked in for the night. Once my eyes adjusted to the gloominess, I quickly found the large ring of rusty iron keys, hanging from a crooked nail.

I held my breath and silently tried the first door, which creaked open to reveal a cobwebbed collection of cardboard boxes. I tried the next door and found a higgledy-piggledy collection of tables and chairs without legs. I continued down the doors until, at last, I found one that was firmly locked.

It took me three keys before I found the right one. The lock clicked. I tucked the keys in my belt, slowly opened the door and peered nervously inside.

Then, in the nick of time, I ducked!

The broken table leg that Mother Hildegard threw furiously at me smashed into the door's edge with a frightening thump.

"Don't you dare come closer, you vagabond!" she growled threateningly.

"OK," I gasped. "I won't."

"Master Jeremiah?" she gasped, dropping her weapon. "Is that you?"

"Yes, Mother Hildegard," I replied nervously.

"What are you doing down here?" she said.

"We're going to escape," I replied. "Nathan, Abby and Suzette are waiting in the orphanage laundry, and if you follow me, we'll hide ourselves in the laundry baskets, and then we ..."

"I'm not hiding in laundry baskets," protested Mother Hildegard. "Bring them here right now."

"But ..."

"Right now," repeated Mother Hildegard in a voice that showed she meant business.

I gulped and, for a fleeting moment, wondered how long it would take to slam the door and turn the key. I knew this had been a bad idea.

3 A Daring Escape

There are some things I never thought I'd see, and the sight of Mother Hildegard's legs, wriggling wildly as she vanished into the darkness of a secret tunnel, was one.

A few moments earlier, Nathan, Abby, Suzette and I had been astonished when Mother Hildegard swung open the door of the cellar next to her temporary prison. After I'd collected the others from the orphanage laundry, we'd raced back to the cellars.

"While I've been locked up next door, I've heard some very strange goings-on," said Mother Hildegard. "I have my suspicions that Father Cicatrice has been engaging in his own grave irregularities."

She pointed to the blocks of stone that had been removed from the wall. Mounds of earth, from a freshly dug tunnel beyond, lay scattered across the cellar floor.

"Where does it lead?" asked Suzette.

“We’re about to find out,” declared Mother Hildegard. And, moments later, I managed to tick off “nun in a tunnel” from my “never-expected-to-see” list.

A muffled voice floated into the cellar. “Are you children coming or not?”

“You first,” I said to Abby. I had little desire to find myself bumping head first into Mother Hildegard’s legs if she slowed down – or worse still, got herself wedged in the tunnel. Nathan, clearly imagining a similar prospect, stood aside in a gentlemanly fashion and waited while Suzette followed Abby.

Nathan and I decided who would be next with a quick “paper, scissors, rock”. I lost, and squirmed into the dark tunnel. It was tight, and for a moment, I wondered how Mother Hildegard had managed to squeeze through. Maybe nuns wore inflatable clothing, like deep-sea divers, and she’d let some of the air out? I mentally added that item to my “hope-I-never-find-out” list. I would have shrugged my shoulders, except there was no room in the tunnel.

I inched forward into the gloom, and then I got the shock of my life.

A hand clenched itself forcefully around my ankle and started pulling me backwards!

"Let go!" I yelled.

The hand locked around my ankle pulled harder! I felt myself being dragged backwards. Suddenly, I popped out of the tunnel, and wriggled around to face my captor.

"Shhh!" hissed Nathan, letting my ankle go. "I thought you should lock Mother Hildegard's cellar door again," he explained. "That way, Father Cicatrice will think she's still trapped."

I took a deep breath, trying to calm my shattered nerves. Nathan was right. I unlooped the keys from my belt, and scurried next door. After a few attempts at finding the right key among the dozen on the keyring, I locked the door and replaced the keys on their original nail.

When I returned, Nathan was nowhere to be seen.

"Come on," came his muffled voice from the tunnel. "We haven't got all night, you know."

But we did have all night – and, like every first glorious night of freedom, it was a night where the stars shone brighter, the air smelled sweeter, and the moon's glow was filled with anticipation.

The tunnel, which wasn't more than ten or eleven metres long, delivered all five of us into a grassy ditch outside the orphanage. From there, we dusted ourselves off and – you guessed it – headed towards the river.

I led the way, the others following quietly. The silence of the night was broken only by the sounds of legs swishing through long, damp grass and clothes brushing against the leaves and brambles of the undergrowth. As we pushed towards the river, we heard the slow-moving water murmuring its welcome.

In the moonlight, I spotted the rotten tree trunk that acted like a slippery bridge. Beyond that, a spooky willow grew right out of the muddy water. I could hardly wait to crawl along its overhanging branch and

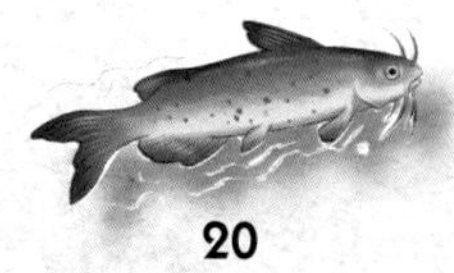

grab the swing rope we'd tied there. Then I stopped, looking back at Mother Hildegard. Would she dare swing herself across the water and crash onto the deck?

She caught my eye and, in an unnerving moment, seemed to read my thoughts. "Don't worry, Master Jeremiah," she sighed, rolling her eyes. "As you may recall, I've done it before."

I sincerely hoped she meant swinging across to the *Zebediah*, not reading my thoughts!

"She caught us on board the *Zebediah* after our last adventure, remember," whispered Nathan.

"That's a relief," I thought to myself. Having a nun know your thoughts would be a truly catastrophic fate too terrible to contemplate!

Two minutes later, I managed to tick something else off my "never-expected-to-see" list: a renegade nun swooping across a moonlit river, letting out a blood-curdling whoop and crashing onto the slippery deck of our secret hideaway, the wreck of the *Zebediah*.

4 A New Crew Member

Nuns, for those of you who have never shared a shipwrecked cabin with them, snore with frightening relish and surprising volume.

My "hope-I-never-find-out" list was growing shorter by the day. As dawn broke, I put down the copy of *The Adventures of Tom Sawyer* that I'd been reading by candlelight since four o'clock and glanced over at Mother Hildegard. She was still snoring fitfully on my bunk bed, while Abby, Suzette and Nathan were huddled asleep under a blanket. I quietly climbed the stairs, and went up to the deck.

I loved the smell of mornings aboard the *Zebediah*. It was as if the world had been freshly laundered, and was slowly drying itself in the first rays of the sun. A flock of terns stood patiently on a rock in the middle of the river, while catfish plopped off the starboard bow.

That made my thoughts turn to breakfast. With the imaginary aroma of catfish sizzling in a frying pan,

I decided to creep downstairs again and search for my trusty fishing line. But someone was already one step ahead of me.

"Morning, Jeremiah," croaked Nathan, his tousled head appearing at the top of the wooden stairs. "I thought we might need these."

"So what now?" he asked, once our lines had plopped into the river, and we'd settled down to contemplate life on the *Zebediah*. "We can't hide out here forever with Mother Hildegard."

"No," I agreed. "I've only got another fifty pages of *Tom Sawyer* left, and that's after a single night of nocturnal nun noises."

"Maybe we should just go to the police station, and tell them the whole story?" suggested Nathan.

Suddenly, there was a noise behind us.

"We can't do that," sighed Mother Hildegard. "I'm afraid Father Cicatrice has already told them his version of the story. That means I'm a fugitive. If the police find me, they'll just lock me up."

The faintest look of delight must have crossed my face because she frowned at me and continued, "And there's no call for celebration, Master Jeremiah. It also means you'll be locked up – for aiding and abetting a fugitive on the run!"

Knowing that Mother Hildegard would, for once, have no chalk to throw at me, I was trying to think of a clever answer – when suddenly there was a sharply satisfying tug on my fishing line.

"Got one!" I cried excitedly. I pulled up a startled-looking catfish just at the moment Nathan blurted out that he had a bite, too.

Mother Hildegard clattered her way hurriedly down into the cabin and reappeared a moment later, holding another fishing line.

"I think you boys could use some help," she declared emphatically. "Move over."

And so we found ourselves, two runaway orphans and a fugitive nun, gleefully hauling up catfish for a delicious breakfast aboard a shipwreck in the middle of a river. My "never-expected-to-see" list was filling up almost as fast as our basket of flapping catfish.

Zebediah

I closed my eyes and took a deep breath of the air below deck, savouring the delicious mixture of water weed, musty blankets and freshly fried catfish. This was just the way life was meant to be – if you didn't count harbouring an escaped fugitive which, I had to admit, added to the feeling of contentment.

Suzette, who had been thumbing through our copy of *The Adventures of Tom Sawyer*, looked up. She had a troubled expression on her face.

"Mother Hildegard," she said hesitantly, "you are innocent, aren't you? You didn't really steal any valuables from the orphanage, did you?"

"Yes dear, and no dear," replied Mother Hildegard, who was trying to dislodge a catfish bone from her teeth in a thoroughly "un-nun-like" manner. "All the orphanage records are kept in meticulous order in my office, and I can assure you there are most definitely no irregularities, grave or otherwise."

"So, how come Father Cicatrice ..."

Mother Hildegard frowned, which may or may not have had anything to do with catfish bone between her teeth.

"I don't know, Suzette," she murmured, shaking her head. "I don't know why he thinks anyone's done anything wrong. In fact, I didn't even know there was an Inspector-General of Irregularities until he turned up that dreadful morning."

"If you're innocent, we have to clear your name, Mother Hildegard," said Abby. "You can't stay a fugitive!"

As long as there were catfish in the river, and as long as I could learn to live with her snoring, I couldn't see why not. I was about to point out that fugitives had much more exciting lives and were generally more famous than people who more or less behaved themselves, when Nathan piped up.

"How can we prove you are innocent?" he mused. "If Father Cicatrice and the police think you're guilty, it's going to be difficult."

Mother Hildegard thought for a moment.

"The only way to demonstrate beyond a doubt that there are no irregularities is to get those records from my office," she said. "But while Father Cicatrice is in charge, that will be impossible."

Poor Mother Hildegard. She'd successfully escaped from the orphanage through a secret tunnel, spent her first night of freedom aboard the *Zebediah* and just eaten a delicious breakfast of freshly caught catfish. And despite all the evidence, she still hadn't realised one very important thing. Aboard the *Zebediah*, nothing was impossible.

5 A Reverse Escape

Against my better judgment, we were about to do the unthinkable. It was something we had never expected to do. Instead of breaking out of the orphanage, Nathan, Abby, Suzette, Mother Hildegard and I were about to do the exact opposite – break in to the orphanage.

For someone who spent most of their daylight hours daydreaming about ways to escape from the orphanage, this was turning out to be a most unusual week!

We'd already revealed our number one escape method, of course, which was hiding amongst the used laundry and waiting for the laundry man to conveniently cart us out on the back of his horse and carriage. We'd never be able to use that trick in future, now that Mother Hildegard knew about it – but, as Abby cleverly pointed out, we could do the reverse. Then, while no one had any inkling that we fugitives and accomplices were inside the orphanage, we could sneak up to Mother Hildegard's office and retrieve the records she needed to prove herself innocent.

As night fell that evening, we made our way off the *Zebediah* and pushed through the undergrowth along the path towards the town, eventually finding ourselves outside the laundry building. The laundry man's horse, which was waiting quietly outside, harrumphed gently, as if to say "haven't seen you for a while". I rubbed its nose, and led Nathan, Abby, Suzette and Mother Hildegard around to the back of the laundry building. There, a door lay ajar, and through it the smell of crisp, clean linen wafted out into the night sky.

I pointed at the carriage parked by the door and climbed aboard. "Come on," I whispered. Within a few seconds, four runaways and a fugitive nun were hidden in wicker baskets, covered with layers of warm, freshly washed and dried laundry. I'd spent plenty of time hidden in baskets of old dirty laundry before, and I must say I was surprised at how pleasant the opposite was by comparison!

We waited in our cocoons of fresh linen, and soon enough, we heard the laundry man lead his obedient horse around the back and hitch it up to the carriage.

With a jolt we were off, rumbling slowly towards the orphanage. After about ten minutes, we stopped, and I knew we had to act quickly!

I threw off the layers of warm linen and clambered out of the basket. The laundry man had hopped off the carriage and was unlocking the orphanage gate, oblivious to what was happening behind him.

"Get ready!" I hissed at the other four baskets clustered next to mine. Like eager pea shoots suddenly popping up from garden pots, four heads emerged from the laundry baskets.

The others climbed out of their baskets, and silently jumped off the carriage. The laundry man, who was concentrating on a jaunty tune he was whistling to himself, climbed back aboard the carriage and moved his load through the gates. In the few seconds it took for him to climb off again and relock the gates behind him, we slipped inside.

We were in. Our reverse escape had worked!

Under the cover of darkness, we hurried as quietly as we could to the main orphanage building and quickly located the door to Mother Hildegard's office.

I'd climbed the stairs to Mother Hildegard's office many times before, of course – usually accompanied by a feeling of foreboding, wondering what kind of miserable punishment she would dish out for my latest misbehaviour. But this time was different. The idea of surreptitiously breaking into Mother Hildegard's office – with Mother Hildegard – was strangely exciting.

Inside the office, Mother Hildegard padded silently towards her mahogany desk. Suddenly, the room was filled with a burst of light and the walls came alive with dancing shadows, as she struck a match.

Within seconds, Mother Hildegard found the lantern she kept on the windowsill, and a warm orange glow filled the room. She gasped.

"The strongbox where I keep all our money and our records," she hissed, "it's empty!" She looked around the room in dismay. "And the irreplaceable gold and silver church ornaments! Gone!"

Nathan, Abby, Suzette and I stared at the empty dust rings that lay everywhere on Mother Hildegard's shelves, and I spotted something on her desk that shouldn't have been there.

On the corner of the desk lay a priest's white dog collar, a pair of spectacles and an unattached moustache!

"Now that is a grave irregularity," I said, staring at the others. "Grave, indeed!"

Nathan gingerly picked up the dog collar.

"It's still warm," he said. "It's only just been taken off. The real criminals must still be in the orphanage!"

"And I know exactly where they'll be!" declared Mother Hildegard emphatically. She whirled around to face me. "Master Jeremiah!" she said. "For once, your knowledge of how to get into places you shouldn't be will come in useful." Her eyes flicked towards Nathan, Abby and Suzette. "And, for once, I will overlook your being accomplices to Master Jeremiah and his dubious skills."

Mother Hildegard quickly outlined her plan, and headed towards the door. "Abby and Suzette," she ordered. "You're coming with me." She stopped and strode back to her desk, scrabbled around urgently in the bottom drawer, and put something into her pocket.

"Now we're ready," she announced, with an alarmingly ferocious smile.

6 Captured!

Nathan and I crept silently down the stairs into the murky darkness of the orphanage cellars, alert for the faintest sound of danger.

We couldn't use a lantern because that would give us away, so we had to feel our way down the stone steps without stumbling. After what seemed like an eternity, we reached the bottom with some relief.

"Jeremiah," started Nathan, but I silenced him with a rapid *shoosh*. Ahead of us, I could see a dull glow coming from one of the cellar doors – the one with the tunnel behind it. Then there was a clatter like stones being dropped and a muffled voice echoed through the darkness.

"HA!" said the voice. "There must be a small fortune here!" There was another clatter, and I realised they weren't stones being dropped. They were coins.

"That's Father Cicatrice," whispered Nathan urgently. "I'd recognise that voice anywhere."

"And," I whispered back, "without the disguise of false spectacles, a dog collar and a moustache, I'd recognise that face anywhere."

A shadow moved in the glow of the cellar, and Father Cicatrice appeared. Except, as I suspected, it wasn't Father Cicatrice.

Nathan's eyes widened like saucers.

"Scarface!" he hissed in disbelief.

I nodded grimly.

"And I'll bet that his usual accomplice, Crooked-Ear, is grinning from ear to crooked ear in that very cell."

A snarling laugh confirmed my suspicions.

"Let's get this lot out of here," growled Crooked-Ear's unpleasant voice from within the cellar. "You go first, and then I'll push the strongbox in behind you. I'll follow, and between us, we'll be able to push and pull it through the tunnel."

I nudged Nathan. "Come on," I said. "They're over here somewhere."

I felt along the cellar wall until my outstretched hand found what I was searching for – the ring of rusty iron keys. Slowly, Nathan and I edged along the cellar

corridor until we dared go no closer to Scarface and Crooked-Ear's cellar.

Suddenly, I had an awful thought, as I fingered the keys in my clammy hand. "There must be at least a dozen," I thought. What if I couldn't find the right one quickly enough? I racked my brain, trying to remember how many I'd tried before finding the one that unlocked Mother Hildegard's cell. Two? Three? Four?

I counted out the keys in my fingers, hoping that whichever nun had looped them on the ring had put them in the correct order of doors.

Two, three or four? I closed my eyes and moved the keys between my fingers. And then the unthinkable happened. I dropped them.

"WHO'S THERE?" roared Scarface from the back of the cellar, where he was preparing to squirm through the tunnel.

There wasn't a second to lose before we were discovered. Nathan darted across the corridor and slammed the cellar door shut with a mighty crash, and I grabbed the ring of keys off the floor and sprinted towards the door. I had no time to count keys.

Scarface and Crooked-Ear would be leaping towards the cellar door. I jammed a key in the lock and turned it.

As Nathan and I stampeded out of the cellars, a furious pounding erupted from the cellar door. We leapt up the stairs, and sprinted for the orphanage gates, desperate to know if the rest of Mother Hildegard's plan was falling into place.

We raced through the gates and dashed around the orphanage wall until we came to the spot where, just one night before, we'd been a fugitive and four runaways tunnelling to freedom. There, we saw Suzette, Abby and Mother Hildegard, while behind them stood a circle of twenty sleepy nuns, hair askew and wearing regulation green orphanage pyjamas

"They looked like a startled bunch of asparagus when we shook them awake," giggled Abby. Suzette was still in a state of shock. She'd never for a moment imagined that nuns ever wore anything but their black and white habits, even to bed.

Mother Hildegard held a finger up to her lips and beckoned for the nuns to crouch down. The nuns fell silent, then noises could be heard coming from the direction of the grassy ditch.

"Pull it harder!" echoed one exasperated voice from the darkness beyond the ditch.

"I am pulling," retorted another muffled, angry voice. "You push it harder!"

Nathan and I exchanged alarmed glances with Abby and Suzette. We'd all heard those voices before – and we knew exactly who they belonged to.

"You two," hissed Mother Hildegard to a pair of nuns at the back of the circle. "Run into town and fetch the police."

Scarface suddenly emerged backwards from the tunnel into the ditch, so intent on hauling the stolen strongbox out of the tunnel that he didn't see the "disapproval" of nuns crouching beyond the ditch.

Mother Hildegard seized the moment. She found a smooth olive-sized pebble on the ground, stood up and, with a look of grim determination, drew out the object she'd hurriedly retrieved from her office earlier.

"That's my slingshot," I gasped, nudging Nathan, "the one Mother Hildegard confiscated last week!"

Mother Hildegard could score a bullseye on a misbehaving orphan with a tiny piece of chalk from across the entire length of a classroom – so a large, wriggling backside jammed into a tunnel was a piece of cake for her.

She stretched back the slingshot elastic as far as she could and let go.

The pebble hummed through the air like a bumblebee on a skyrocket and a split second later found its target!

"OWWW!" screamed Scarface. He instinctively jerked his head up and whacked the roof of the tunnel. "OWWW!" he repeated painfully.

"Wow!" I breathed in admiration. She was good.

"Don't move a muscle, Father Cicatrice," snorted Mother Hildegard, using the criminal's alias. "Next time, I won't use a smooth pebble, but one covered with irregularities – sharp, pointy irregularities. Would you like to inspect them?"

"No, no, no," whimpered Scarface, who knew he was in no position to argue.

"The door's locked behind them," I called out. "There's no escape."

Mother Hildegard nodded in my direction. "Good," she said with a satisfied smile. "Now we just need to wait for the police to arrive." Her fingers scrabbled around the ground, until they closed over a smooth, round pebble. She handed it, and the slingshot, to me.

"If you thieves move or try anything nefarious, this boy has my permission to use your posterior for target practice," she declared, with a meaningful wink in my direction.

It was probably about the last thing I'd get to cross off my "never-expected-to-see" list for a while: a winking ex-fugitive nun handing me a slingshot and a pebble, and pointing at a large, trapped backside. Life sure had been peculiar these last few days.

7 Epilogue

When the police arrived and hustled Scarface and Crooked Ear away, I toyed with the idea of slipping back to the *Zebediah* under cover of darkness, but unfortunately Mother Hildegard was having none of that.

"Master Jeremiah, Nathan, Abby, Suzette!" she said, casting a quivering eyebrow in our direction. "My office. Now!"

My heart sank. We trudged back inside the orphanage and up the stairs to her office, waiting for Mother Hildegard to join us.

"This time we only had one night and day aboard the *Zebediah*," I said glumly, looking around at the others. "And now we're back here."

"But it was a fun night and day," piped up Suzette. "I think Mother Hildegard quite enjoyed it. She escaped through a secret tunnel, slept in an old bunk bed, watched the sun rise over the river, caught catfish

for breakfast, and smuggled herself into the orphanage hidden in laundry!"

"I never expected to see Mother Hildegard doing those things," said Abby, shaking her head and trying not to grin.

"She was a pretty mean shot with that slingshot, Jeremiah," observed Nathan.

Even I had to admit he was right. I knew Mother Hildegard could be dangerous with a piece of chalk, but I'd have to be extra careful to pay attention in class now, after seeing how accurate she could be with something much more painful.

We heard the ominous clumping of a nun's boots climbing the stairs, and Mother Hildegard strode through the doorway. She took her seat behind the desk and looked at us sternly.

"Despite the circumstances of the last few days, I can't be seen to be allowing children in this orphanage to escape whenever they feel like it."

"But," I started to protest, but Mother Hildegard silenced me with a crooked finger.

"Let me finish, Master Jeremiah. Much as it pains me, I have decided what your punishment will be."

After all we'd done to help her, we were about to be punished. I couldn't believe it. I knew I should have ignored my conscience when I'd had the chance, right at the beginning of the adventure.

"It's Friday night," continued Mother Hildegard. "You are all hereby suspended until Monday morning."

"Suspended?" said Suzette, looking horrified. "What does that mean?"

"It means you are banned from attending this orphanage until Monday morning," said Mother Hildegard with an exasperated frown.

"But where are we supposed to go?" asked Abby. Then she smiled, as it dawned on her what Mother Hildegard was really saying.

"Can I have my slingshot back?" I asked hopefully. It would be quite useful to have during the free weekend Mother Hildegard was about to give us aboard the *Zebediah*.

"Don't push your luck," she snapped back. "And if you're not all back here first thing on Monday, there really will be trouble," she added, looking directly at me.

Suzette, who'd finally realised what was going on, smiled at Mother Hildegard. "It won't be the same without our fugitive stowaway on board," she chuckled. "You were quite good at swinging across on the rope, catching catfish and being on the run from the orphanage."

"I may have lived most of my life here," commented Mother Hildegard mysteriously, "but it wasn't always as a nun."

I had no idea what she was talking about, because I was daydreaming of two perfect days, free to do whatever I pleased aboard the *Zebediah*.

And while, at that moment, I knew my "never-expected-to-see" list was about as complete as it ever would be, it took me a long, long time to figure out exactly what Mother Hildegard was saying about her past, the *Zebediah*, and the excitement of childhood days spent roaming free.

As usual, my mind was elsewhere!